D1299121

3181

THE ADVENTURES OF

Jack and Rugby

THE BIG TRIP

STORY AND PHOTOGRAPHS BY

TORY BEALE • **CYNTHIA MESSER**

Tory Beale
Cynthia Messer

Text and photographs copyright © 2011 Tory Beale and Cynthia Messer
First edition January, 2011
All rights reserved. No part of this book may be reproduced in any form without written permission from the authors.
Library of Congress Cataloging-in-publication Data available.
ISBN 978-1-935530-31-2 Library of Congress Control Number: 2010942228
Printed in China
Published by Park Place Publications, Pacific Grove, CA *www.parkplacepublications.com*
Book design in collaboration with Sandy Frye *www.sandyfrye.com*
www.jackandrugby.com

Meet Jack and Rugby

Jack is a medium-sized Labrador Retriever. His fur is smooth and shiny. He is full of energy, very alert, and sometimes a little worried. He wonders what's happening next, doesn't like loud noises, and is usually too busy to take a nap.

Rugby is an enormous Poodle. His fur is soft and curly. His head is as high as a doorknob! He is fluffy, floppy, and happy-go-lucky. He is so easy-going, nothing worries him. After playing, he loves to cuddle up and have a nice snooze.

Jack and Rugby are best friends.

Jack was very excited.

His best friend, Rugby, arrived at his house early this morning
and now there was a great commotion around Jack's car.

Something unusual was happening.

Jack ran over and looked inside. "Hey, Rugby! My skunk's in the car!
Do you see that? Stinky's in the car!"

Rugby peered in. "How about that, Jack? My Mousie's in the car, too!
And our bowls, and our food, and our sleeping blankets!
Hey, that's all our stuff. Maybe we're going on a trip! Quick, let's get in!"

The car pulled away from Jack's house and they drove for a long time.

The car climbed higher and higher and the road twisted and turned.

Rugby fell asleep.

Jack was getting restless.

He stuck his head out the window and smelled the fresh scent of a pine forest.

He poked Rugby. "Wake up! Do you think we're in the mountains? I've never been to the mountains before!"

Rugby sat up and sniffed. "These *are* the mountains, Jack! Look, we're stopping!"

The tall mountains were the California Sierras, and they had arrived at Gray Eagle Lodge.

Jack and Rugby saw lots of little cabins nestled in the woods.

The dogs jumped out and ran to find their cabin.

They saw a perfect one hidden behind some trees at the edge of a beautiful meadow.

They pushed open the door and looked inside.

"Can we stay in this one? It's really cool!"

Jack and Rugby chose their beds, and carried Mousie and Stinky in from the car.

After unpacking, there was still time before dark to go exploring.
The two friends set off with their noses to the ground.

Rugby's nose led him to a big, old tree stump.
"Do you smell what I smell, Jack?"

Suddenly there was a chattering sound from above their heads.

A little chipmunk was keeping watch from his lookout.

He called to the two dogs.

"Do you want to play hide-and-seek, hide-and-seek?"

"Hey, Jack, did you hear that?"

Rugby tried to climb up to see who was calling to them.

As his huge head peered over the stump, the chipmunk darted past him up the tree. "I saw him, Jack! Where did he go?"

"Chee chee chee! Here I am!
Here I am!"

Jack thought his friend was imagining
things. "Let's go, Rugby. There's
nothing there."

Jack ran off across the meadow.

Rugby climbed higher up the stump.
"I *know* it was here."

The chipmunk darted into the woods.

"See you later! See you later!"

Just then Rugby heard a splash.

He ran to the edge of the meadow and looked down.

"Where are you, Jack?"

Jack came swimming by.

"Look, Rugby, a river! Jump in!"

Rugby was thirsty, but he didn't feel like getting wet.

He carefully held on with his hind legs, trying not to slip into the river, while he slurped the cool water.

Then he lay down in the shade and watched Jack swim and collect sticks.

The sun was going down and the mountain air suddenly felt cold.

Jack was chilly and wet, and Rugby felt cold, too.

They ran into their cabin and sat by a crackling fire in the fireplace.

Soon they were toasty and warm.

Jack began to think about his soft blanket and wondered if his cuddle baby, Stinky, was feeling lonely. "Rugby, let's get cozy on our beds and play with our toys."

Jack found Stinky sitting on his bed. The skunk didn't seem lonely at all, so Jack hopped up on Rugby's bed and squeaked Mousie. "Let's trade beds, Rugby."

Rugby agreed sleepily, and he climbed up onto Jack's bed, snuggling up with Stinky. "Goodnight, Jack." Rugby put his head down and was soon fast asleep.

Jack played a little longer, chewing softly on Rugby's mouse, and soon he fell asleep, too.

The next day the friends woke up early and ran outside.

The river sparkled in the morning sun.

Rugby looked across to the other side. "I wonder what's over there, Jack."

Jack was ready to swim across.

But Rugby, who was not fond of swimming, ran along the riverbank.
"Look, Jack! A bridge!"

They trotted onto the bridge and stopped in the middle.

They could see a wild forest on the other side.

Rugby looked up. A huge mountain loomed in the distance.
"Let's climb to the top of that mountain, Jack!"

Jack suddenly sat down.

"It's so far away, Rugby…There might be bears up there. Let's just stay here and swim."

"C'mon, Jack. I'm not afraid of bears, and it will be fun. We'll find some sticks and some squirrels to chase."

Jack felt braver knowing he'd be with his big friend, Rugby. He stood up and they continued across the bridge.

On the other side, they spotted a path that disappeared into the forest.

Jack looked back at the river and their cabin. "What if we get lost, Rugby?"

"Don't worry, Jack. We'll stay on the trail, and we'll be back before dark. C'mon!"

Rugby dashed up the trail and Jack followed.

Along the way, they came to a shallow stream that they had to cross.

They stopped to play in the cool water.

Jack found a stick. "You were right, Rugby.
Hiking in the mountains is fun! What did you find?"

Rugby was pawing the water. "I almost caught a fish!"

Jack found a trail on the other side of the stream.

There was a new smell ahead and the two friends raced up the path.

They rounded the bend and came to a clearing in the forest.

They stopped and were silent. They could hardly believe their eyes.

It was the biggest lake they had ever seen.

Jack saw something floating in the lake.

"Let's go swimming, Rugby!"

He waded into the water
and started to paddle out.

Rugby started to follow Jack into the water, but he stopped.

He was happier when his feet could touch the bottom.

Jack kept swimming. He was getting farther and farther from the shore.

Rugby wondered if he should get help.

Jack was coming back!
"Look what I caught, Rugby. Another stick!"

"That's cool, Jack. You're such a good swimmer!"

Jack came splashing out of the lake. "That felt great. Here, I'll cool you off."

Jack shook water all over his friend.

Then he bounded away.

"Bet you can't catch me, Rugby!"

Rugby chased after Jack …

and Jack turned and raced after Rugby.

The lake didn't seem so big when you were with your best friend.

Rugby stretched out on a warm rock.

Jack sat close to his friend and gazed at the lake.
"I'm happy, Rugby."

"Me too, Jack."

Suddenly they were
startled by a loud
rustling in the bushes.

Was it a deer?

Was it a bear?

They followed the sound deep
into the forest.

Jack heard something run up a tree.

He looked around for Rugby.

It was dark and shadowy.

He didn't see Rugby anywhere.

Shivers ran down his back.
"Rugby, are you here?"

Jack saw something big and black in the shadows,
with its head hidden in a hollow log.

He started to tremble. It must be a bear!

Just then, Rugby pulled his head out of the hole in the log.
"It's just me, Jack. I almost caught a raccoon!"

Jack quickly ran out of the forest into the sunshine and Rugby followed.
"That was scary, Rugby. I want to go back now."

"But we haven't gotten to the top of the mountain yet, Jack.
Let's go just a little farther. I won't leave you this time."

They climbed higher and higher, and the trail got steeper and dustier.

Hot and thirsty, they finally reached the top of the mountain.

Rugby stood tall. "We're the kings of the mountain!"

Jack felt proud. He stood on a rock and looked at the view.

He saw something sparkling in the distance.
"Look, Rugby, another lake!"

"Let's go!"

Jack plunged into the cool water.

Rugby was so hot and thirsty that he followed Jack into the lake.

Jack looked back at his friend. "Rugby, look, you're swimming!"

Jack and Rugby played in the lake, leaping over logs and splashing each other happily.

Rugby paused to take a big
drink of lake water.

"I think I like swimming, Jack.
Let's swim some more!"

Jack remembered that it was getting late.

"We'd better go, Rugby. It'll be dark soon."

They said good-bye to the lake and began the long hike back to the cabin.

After a while, Jack realized he didn't hear Rugby's footsteps behind him.

He turned around.

Rugby was sound asleep in the middle of the path.

"Rugby! C'mon! We've got to keep walking!"

Rugby rolled over and started to snore.

Jack was stern with his friend. "Look, Rugby, this is serious. We have to keep going or it will be dark, and we won't be able to find our way back to the cabin."

Rugby slowly got up.

Jack decided to follow Rugby this time, in case his friend decided to take another nap.

They crossed the bridge at Gray Eagle Lodge
just before the sun disappeared behind the mountains.

The tired friends reached their cabin. They saw their car packed and ready for the long drive home.

It was time to say good-bye to Gray Eagle Lodge.

Jack and Rugby slowly climbed into the car, taking a few pinecones and sticks for souvenirs.

As the car began to wind down the mountain, the two friends felt drowsy.

Jack fell asleep with his head on Stinky, and soon was dreaming of lakes and sticks.

Rugby softly laid his head on Mousie, with sleepy memories of chasing chipmunks and climbing tall mountains.

This had been a very big trip.

Meet the Authors

Tory Beale, an artist and former child therapist, lives with her family in La Selva Beach, California. Cynthia Messer lives with her family in Soquel, California, and is an educator and child advocate. Their friendship began with the scheduling of puppy play dates, and, as their dogs became best friends, so did they.

These stories grew out of their delightful excursions and real adventures with Jack and Rugby.

Our Special Gratitude:

To our loving husbands, Rich and Teall, for being so generous with their time, their enthusiasm, their patience and humor. To our children, Ari, Sophie, Scott, and Greg, for their constructive feedback, for cheering us on, and for never being jealous of their brothers, Jack and Rugby. To Sandy Frye, for her design expertise, invaluable suggestions, and love of dogs, and with whom it's been a pleasure to work. To Patricia Hamilton, for her patient guidance and her professional knowledge of the publishing world.

And most importantly, to dear Jack and Rugby, for bringing us such joy and delight, and for being our best friends forever.